Pocket Scientist
FLIGHT &
FLOATING

Illustrat

Science Consultant: Dr M. P. Hollins
Editor: Helen Davies

Contents

First published in 1981 by
Usborne Publishing Ltd,
20 Garrick Street,
London WC2E 9BJ, England.

Copyright © 1981 Usborne
Publishing Ltd

GRÁFICAS REUNIDAS, S. A.
Av. de Aragón, 56.— Madrid-27.

We are grateful to John Murray (Publishers) Ltd for permission
to reproduce Barnaby's glider (pages 28–31) from "How to make and fly
paper aircraft" by Barnaby.

About this book

This book is full of experiments to help you find out how things fly and float. There are lots of models to make too, and ideas for testing them to see how they work. The first part is about flight and the second about floating.

With each model or experiment there is an explanation to show how it works. You can find out how real things, such as submarines and helicopters, work too.

Over the page there is a list of the main things you need for the models and experiments and some hints on how to make them successful.

There are lots of puzzles to do, which you can solve by experimenting. You can check your results with the answers on page 61.

3

Being a scientist

When you build a model, or do an experiment, you need to be careful and accurate, as a real scientist would be. On these two pages there are some hints on being a scientist. If you follow these, your projects should be successful, though even real scientists sometimes have to repeat experiments because they do not work first time.

It is a good idea to start collecting equipment. You can find most of the things you need around the house. Put them in an old box, or if you have a shed, you could make it your "laboratory".

USEFUL THINGS

PAPER
PENCIL
RULER
FELT-TIP PEN
SCISSORS
STICKY TAPE
GLUE
PLASTICINE
CANDLE

DRINKING STRAW
PAPER-CLIPS
STRING
COTTON REELS
EMPTY PLASTIC BOTTLE
NAILS
JAM JARS

Getting ready

Collect everything you need before you start. If you do not have one thing, try and think of something else you can use.

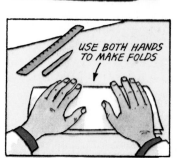

USE BOTH HANDS TO MAKE FOLDS

When you are making models, measure or trace lines accurately. Be especially careful to make folds smooth and even.

Hints for doing tests

Set tests up carefully, as the conditions in the room can affect the results. Make sure draughts do not spoil flight tests and that water is deep enough for floating.

Before you do an experiment, try to guess what will happen. Then you can do the experiment to see if your idea was right. Do not look at the explanation first.

Watch tests closely. Sometimes things will happen very quickly, so you have to concentrate hard. Repeat a test several times to be sure the result is not a fluke.

If your results are different from those in the book, it does not mean they are wrong. See if you can work out what happened and then try some tests to check your idea.

Finding out more

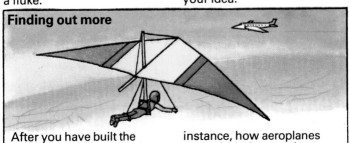

After you have built the models in this book, you should have a good idea how things fly and float. They will help you understand, for instance, how aeroplanes and submarines work. Maybe you can invent models of other things, such as hang-gliders and kites.

Falling and floating

The experiments on this page are about falling. Things fall because they are pulled towards the Earth by a force called gravity.

You can find out more about gravity by doing the test on the right.

You can find out more about gravity by doing the test on the right.

1 Gravity test

Screw up a piece of paper and find a heavy stone. Drop both from the same height, at the same moment, and note when they land.

2

The ball of paper lands at the same time as the stone, even though it is much lighter. This is because the pull of gravity is the same on all objects, no matter how heavy.

Another way of falling

Have you ever watched falling leaves and conkers, though, on a still day? The conkers fall straight to the ground, but the leaves float down slowly. Can you think why this should be?

Experiment

Take two pieces of paper and crumple one into a ball, as you did before.

Drop them from the same height, at the same moment, and watch when they land.

Try it several times. Why do you think the flat paper always falls more slowly?

Why it happens

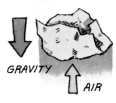

GRAVITY

AIR

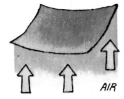

AIR

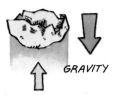

GRAVITY

As the papers fall, air is trapped and squashed under them. This air presses up against them and stops them falling so fast. The flat paper falls more slowly than the crumpled one because it has a larger area, so more air is trapped underneath it. This is also why the large, flat leaves fall more slowly than the conkers.

Trick your friends

HEAVY

Tear two pages from a notebook, and write the word "HEAVY" on one. Ask some friends if they can work out how to drop the papers from the same height, at the same time, and make the "HEAVY" one land first. (Answer: crumple the "HEAVY" paper so it traps less air.)

Making parachutes

The modern parachute was invented in 1797 by André–Jacques Garnerin. He jumped out of a hot air balloon and, wearing his parachute, floated safely to the ground. His daughter, Eliza, was the first woman parachutist.

To make some paper parachutes, you need tissue paper, sticky tape, thread and paper-clips.

To make two parachutes, one slightly larger than the other, cut two squares of tissue paper, one 30cm×30cm and one 20cm×20cm.

Tape threads, about 15cm long, to each corner of each piece of paper.

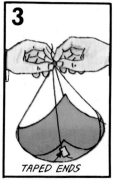

TAPED ENDS

Tie the threads like this, with the taped ends on the outside of the parachute.

Hook two paper-clips on to each parachute, so both have an equal load.

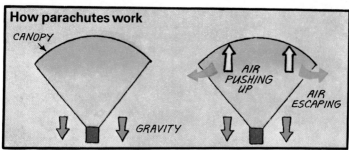

How parachutes work

CANOPY

AIR PUSHING UP

AIR ESCAPING

GRAVITY

Gravity pulls the parachute down, but as it falls, air is trapped under the canopy. The air gets squashed up or compressed, and pushes up against the canopy, making the parachute fall slowly.

5

To test the parachutes, drop them from the top of the stairs, or stand on a chair. Why do you think one of the parachutes takes longer to fall? See what happens if you hook on more paper-clips.

Experiment

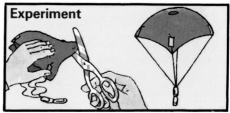

The trapped air escapes unevenly from under the canopy, and makes the parachute sway. Try cutting a hole in the top, to see if it helps to stop this.

Garnerin's parachute

Garnerin's parachute wobbled badly as the trapped air escaped in sudden spurts from either side of the canopy. This made him feel very sick, so he made a hole in the top of the canopy to let the air escape more smoothly. All modern parachutes have a hole at the top.

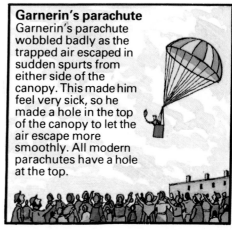

Paper helicopters

These two pages show you how to make a paper helicopter. Then, over the page, there are some helicopter experiments and a game to play.

Cut a piece of paper so it measures 20cm×7cm. Then make three cuts in it, as shown.

FOLD   BEND

Fold over the two sides below the cuts, to make a thin strip. Bend the end of the strip up.

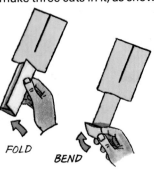

Fold the two strips at the top out as shown, to make the rotors which make the helicopter spin.

Flight test
Now stand on a chair and drop the helicopter. Watch how it takes a second or two to start spinning.

Puzzles
1. Can you make another helicopter, out of the same sized paper, which falls more quickly? You will need to alter the design slightly (Answer on page 61.)
2. How can you make the helicopter spin round the other way? You can find out in the explanation on the opposite page, but try to work it out first.

10

Why the helicopter spins

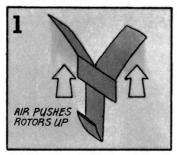

AIR PUSHES
ROTORS UP

As the paper helicopter falls, air is trapped under the rotors. The pressure of the air pushes the rotors up in a slanting position.

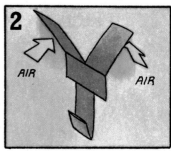

AIR

AIR

In this position, the air under one rotor is pushing one way and the air under the other rotor is pushing the opposite way.

HELICOPTER
SPINNING
AS IT FALLS

Now, as the helicopter falls, the two forces of air push the rotors round and make it spin.

Try bending the rotors back in the opposite direction and see what happens.

Now the forces of air push the other way and the helicopter spins in the opposite direction.

Flying top
Spinning keeps the helicopter upright and stops it toppling over as it falls. In the same way, a spinning top can balance on its end.

Paper helicopter experiments

Try dropping a paper helicopter upside-down. Does it turn up the right way again?

What happens if you cut off half of one of the rotors?

Now cut one rotor off completely. Do you think the helicopter will still spin?

Watch carefully how it falls. Air presses against the base of the rotor, so there are still two forces of air making it spin.

What happens if you cut the base of the rotor off too? Can you think of other tests to try out on the helicopter?

Sycamore helicopters

The seed of a sycamore fruit has only one wing and it spins like a helicopter with one rotor. On one side, air pushes against the wing and on the other side, against the seed. As it falls, only the wing seems to be spinning, but here is a test to show that both ends spin.

WING

SEED

Paint a white spot at each end of a sycamore fruit. Drop it and watch it spin.

Two white circles appear, showing that both ends of the fruit move round.

Helicopter game

For this game you need to make a target as shown below and some helicopters. Then take it in turns to bomb the target. You can make up your own rules, or use these: score two points for a bull's eye, one for inside the circle, and lose one if you miss altogether.

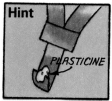

Hint

PLASTICINE

If no-one can hit the bull's eye, try weighting each helicopter with a small piece of plasticine.

BULL'S EYE

Making the target

Put a large plate on a big piece of paper and draw round it to make a circle.

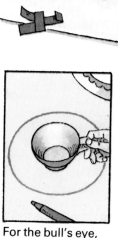

For the bull's eye, put a cup in the middle of the circle.

Make three helicopters for each player.

Vertical take-off helicopter

Try making this helicopter
which lifts itself up off a
launching pad.

You need a piece of card about
20cm×20cm (the back of a
cereal packet would do), tracing
paper, pencil, ruler, paper-clips
and a thin, plastic cotton reel.

For the launching pad you need
a stick, such as a paintbrush
handle, narrow enough to slip
through the cotton reel, and
some string.

How to make the helicopter

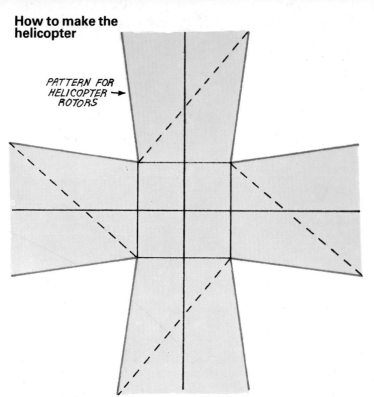

PATTERN FOR HELICOPTER ROTORS →

You must have this pattern the right way round, so trace it, then scribble on the back of the tracing. Put it the right way up on the centre of the card, then draw over the lines again.

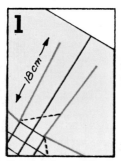

1

18cm

Extend the red lines until they each measure 18cm.

2

Join the tops of the red lines to make the rotors.

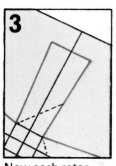

3

Now each rotor should look like this.

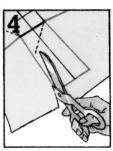

Cut round the rotors following the lines carefully.

Turn the card over and glue the cotton reel in the middle where the rotors meet. Use a strong, all-purpose glue and leave it to dry for a few hours so it is firmly stuck.

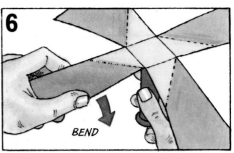

BEND

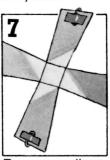

Bend the rotors down along the dotted lines, as shown. This is very important – it makes the rotors slant, so one edge is lower than the other. Take care not to break the card.

Tape paper-clips to the ends of two rotors which are opposite each other.

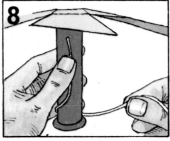

UPPER EDGE

WIND THIS WAY

Now wind the string round the cotton reel. Hold one end along the reel, to catch it in, and start winding from the bottom.

Make sure you wind the string so it goes round towards the upper edge of each rotor. It should go round 15 times.

Lift off

1

Holding the string tight, put the cotton reel on to the end of the stick.

2

Hold the stick in one hand and the string in the other, as shown.

3

Then pull the string firmly and steadily, until it comes right off the reel. The helicopter should spin up into the air. You can find out how it works on the next page.

Launching hints

Make sure you have wound the string towards the upper edge of each rotor.

Check that the rotors are bent down properly.

Try slanting the stick slightly, and make sure you do not jerk the string.

How a helicopter takes off

Your model helicopter takes off in a similar way to a real one. On both, the rotors spinning round lift the helicopter into the air. The rotors are driven round by the engine on a real helicopter. On the model, you pull the string to make them spin.

1

ROTORS GO THIS WAY

FRONT EDGE

AIR

2

AIR PUSHES UP

Helicopter rotors are slanted, so the front edge is higher than the back. As they turn, the front edge cuts into the air and forces it down under the back edge.

The more the rotors spin, the more air is pushed down and the pressure of the air under the rotors pushes the helicopter up.

18

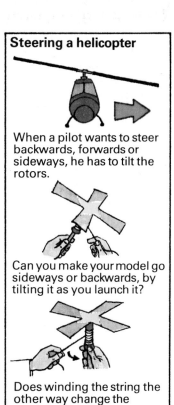

When a pilot wants to steer backwards, forwards or sideways, he has to tilt the rotors.

Can you make your model go sideways or backwards, by tilting it as you launch it?

Does winding the string the other way change the model's flight?

3

The rotors of the model are bent so they work in the same way. Air is pressed down and the increased pressure under the model pushes it up into the air.

4

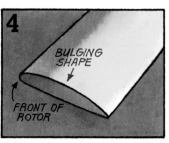

BULGING SHAPE

FRONT OF ROTOR

Helicopter rotors are a special bulging shape and this also helps them to fly. You can find out about this on page 34.

19

How to make paper fly

On these two pages you can find out how to make a sheet of paper into a simple glider. You need a piece of paper about 20cm×25cm.

First see what happens if you drop the paper flat, like this. It sways from side to side and may even flip right over. You need to find a way to make it glide forward and fall smoothly.

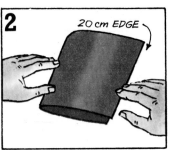

20 cm EDGE

Fold the paper in half as shown. Then open it out and drop it as before. The crease should stop it swaying from side to side.

MAKE SURE FOLD IS NEAT AND EVEN

To make it go forward, try making one end heavier. Fold one long edge back about 1.5cm. Drop the paper again.

Keep folding the edge over, 1.5cm at a time, and testing the paper until the front edge is heavy enough and the paper glides forward.

What is happening

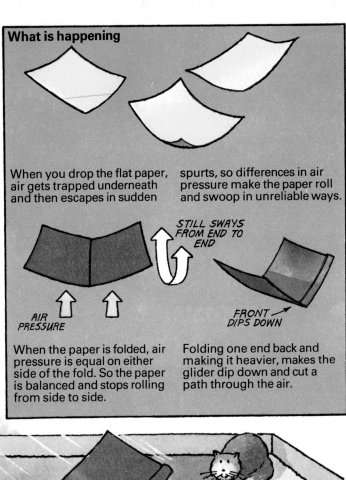

When you drop the flat paper, air gets trapped underneath and then escapes in sudden spurts, so differences in air pressure make the paper roll and swoop in unreliable ways.

STILL SWAYS FROM END TO END

AIR PRESSURE

FRONT DIPS DOWN

When the paper is folded, air pressure is equal on either side of the fold. So the paper is balanced and stops rolling from side to side.

Folding one end back and making it heavier, makes the glider dip down and cut a path through the air.

If you fold the paper too many times the glider will dive sharply because the front is too heavy. If you do not fold it enough, the glider will lurch up and down. Keep experimenting until the weight is right and it glides smoothly.

Glider flight research

Here are some tests to find
out how to control the glider
on page 20 and make it
fly in the direction you
want. To do this you
need flaps, called
elevons, in the back
edge. You can find out
how to cut them below.

ELEVON
FLAPS

It is best to do the tests in a
room with no draughts, as these may blow the glider off
course. Close doors and windows and keep away from
heaters which create air currents. Clear an open space so the
glider does not crash into things.

How to make elevons

Fold the glider in
half and make two
cuts, 2cm deep and
5cm apart as shown.

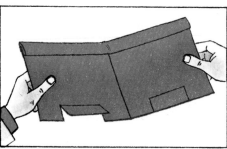

Open the glider out and bend one elevon
up. To test the glider, hold it in both hands
and drop it. Then see what happens if you
bend up the other elevon instead.

How elevons work

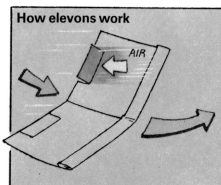

AIR

Air flows smoothly
over the glider until it
hits the elevon which is
sticking up. The air
presses against the
elevon flap and this
slows that wing down.
Now one wing is
moving faster than the
other and this makes
the whole glider swing
round.

Flight tests

Now see how many different directions you can make the glider fly in. The glider works best if you launch it instead of dropping it, and you can find out how to do that here.

How to launch

How to hold the glider

For a smooth launch, it is important to hold the glider in the right way. Hold the back edge loosely between your thumb and fingers as shown. It is like holding a pencil.

Hold the glider at shoulder height and, aiming slightly downwards, push it gently into the air. If it does not work very well at first you are probably pushing too hard.

Aerobatic puzzles

You can make the glider do all sorts of things by bending the elevons up or down and launching it at different angles.

See if you can work out how to make it do the following:
1. Loop the loop.
2. Dive and turn upside-down.
3. Turn sharply left or right.

(Answers on page 61.)

Mark 2 glider

Here is another glider to make. It has wings and a tail, like an aeroplane. There are two sets of control flaps, one on the wings and one on the tail. These do the same job as elevons, but in a different way.

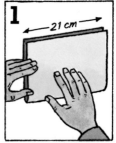

1

← 21 cm →

Fold in half a sheet of paper measuring at least 21cm×30cm, as shown here.

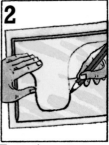

2

Trace the pattern on page 62 on to one side of the folded paper.

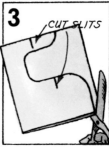

3

CUT SLITS

Cut round the pattern through both thicknesses of paper, and cut the slits too.

4

Then open the paper out and fold the front edge back 1.5cm. Test it, and keep on folding and testing it until it flies smoothly.

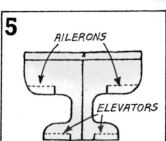

5

AILERONS

ELEVATORS

Now fold back the edges of the wings and tail to make flaps. The wing flaps are ailerons and the tail flaps are elevators.

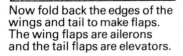

Making the glider turn

Ailerons make the glider turn left or right. See what happens if you bend the left one up and the right one down. Then try them the other way round.

Climbing and diving

Elevators make the glider dive or climb. What happens when you bend both up and drop the glider nose first?

Then try bending both elevators down and launching the glider horizontally.

Over the page you can find out how flight controls work.

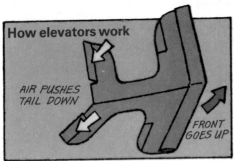

How elevators work

AIR PUSHES TAIL DOWN

FRONT GOES UP

AIR PUSHES UP

When both elevators are up, air trapped against them pushes the glider's tail down. This makes the front go up and so the glider climbs.

When both elevators are down, air pushes the tail up and the glider dives.

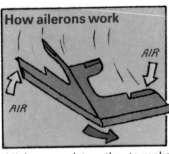

How ailerons work

AIR

AIR

Ailerons work together to make the glider turn. Trapped air pushes the wing with the raised flap down and the other wing

up. This tilts the glider and makes it swing round. When the left flap is up it turns to the left. It turns right with the right one up.

How aeroplanes turn

TAILPLANE

RUDDER

To turn, aircraft use a tail flap called the rudder, as well as ailerons. To turn right, the rudder is bent right. Air pressing against it pushes the

tail to the left and the plane swings round to the right. The ailerons make the plane tilt as it turns. This is called banking and it helps the plane to turn.

26

High-speed flight controls

Planes which are designed for high-speed flight, such as *Concorde*, have special triangular-shaped wings. They are called delta wings after the Greek letter "delta" which is written like this △.

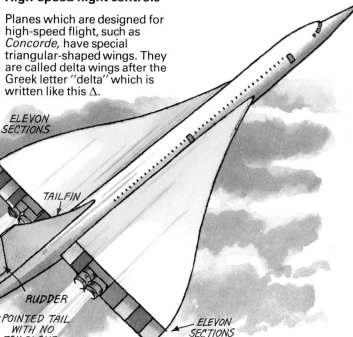

ELEVON SECTIONS

TAILFIN

RUDDER

POINTED TAIL WITH NO TAILPLANE

ELEVON SECTIONS

Delta-winged aircraft have a tailfin, but no tailplane, so they cannot have separate ailerons and elevators. Instead they have elevons, like the glider on page 22, which do the job of both. *Concorde* has three elevon sections on each wing.

Using elevons

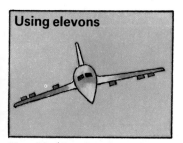

To make the plane bank for a turn, the elevons are raised on one side and lowered on the other, like ailerons.

To climb and turn right, the rudder is bent right and the right elevons raised. The left ones are kept level.

Make and fly a superglider

In 1967 a "Great International Paper Airplane Competition" was held in America. One of the winning gliders was made by Ralph Barnaby. He used to make paper gliders while on ballooning trips in the 1920s, and test them by dropping them from the balloon. Often he could see them circling below for 20 minutes before they disappeared from sight. Here is a glider, like Barnaby's winner, for you to make.

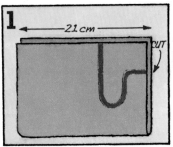

You need a piece of paper measuring 21cm×30cm, folded as shown. Draw a pattern on it, like the one here, and cut it out.

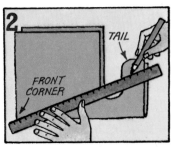

Place a ruler over the front corner and across the tail like this. Draw a line on the tail only, as shown in the picture.

3

Bend out one side of the tail along the line you have drawn.

4

Bend out the other side in the same way, using the first fold as a guide.

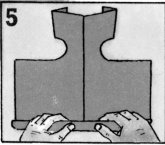

5

Open the glider out and fold back the front edge, like this, until the wings are about half their original size.

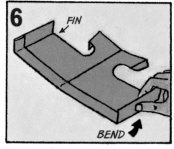

6

FIN

BEND

Bend up about 2cm at the tip of each wing, to make "fins". These help to keep the glider on a straight course.

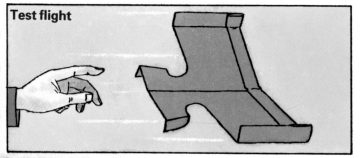

Test flight

Now test the superglider, launching it as shown for the glider on page 23.

If it does not fly very well you can find out how to improve it over the page.

Improving the superglider

Here are some ways to improve the glider if it does not fly very well at first.

1. If the glider dives
Try cutting elevators* in the tail and bending them up.

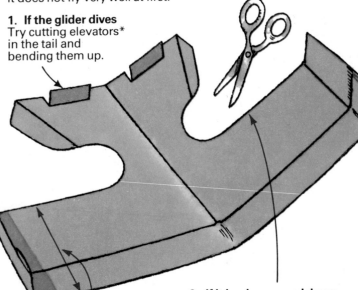

2. If it still dives
The front is too heavy. Try folding the front edge back less. Or you may have to make a new glider, with a broader wing.

3. If it lurches up and down
It may help to cut a thin strip off the back edge of the wings. Fold the glider and trim both wings together, so they are the same. Trim the glider until it flies really well.

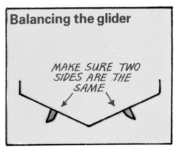

Balancing the glider

MAKE SURE TWO SIDES ARE THE SAME

If it swerves, the glider may not be properly balanced. Look at it head on and push the wings up or down to make them level.

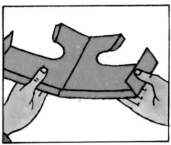

If it still swerves, you may need to bend one of the fins in further than the other. Adjust the fins until it flies straight.

* You can find out about elevators on pages 24–26.

Fast launch

Here is a special launch which makes the glider go very fast. Hold the front edge between your finger and thumb, with your hand underneath the glider, as shown on the right. Then move your hand forward fast. Let go almost immediately and pull your hand out of the way.

If you launch the glider like this and throw it up steeply, it should loop the loop. It may take a bit of practice to do this.

A flying competition

Can you invent some more glider designs? You could have a competition to see whose glider flies the furthest when launched from the same height, or whose glider is best at looping the loop.

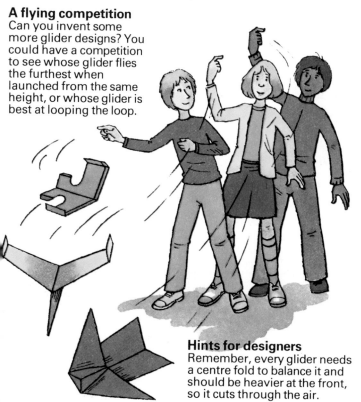

Hints for designers

Remember, every glider needs a centre fold to balance it and should be heavier at the front, so it cuts through the air.

Lifting things on air

On these two pages there are lots of tricks you can do, making things rise up and hover in the air. All these tricks are based on a scientific discovery made in 1738, by a Swiss scientist called Bernoulli. Bernoulli found that moving air has less pressure than the still air around it. This is called the Bernoulli principle.

1 Paper strip trick

Cut a strip of paper and hold one end against your chin, just below your bottom lip. Then blow straight ahead.

2

The paper should lift up and flutter about, as it is sucked into the air stream of your breath.

3 Why it happens

LOW PRESSURE

The moving air of your breath has less pressure than the still air below the paper.

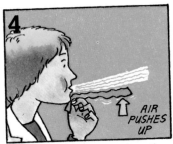

4

AIR PUSHES UP

The still air pushes up into the low pressure area and lifts the paper up with it.

How planes fly

The Bernoulli principle also explains how planes can fly. You can find out about this over the page.

Jumping coin trick

TRAPPED AIR PUSHES UP

Put a saucer about 10cm from the edge of a table and lay a small coin in front.

Rest your bottom lip against the table edge and blow across the top of the coin.

Air trapped under the coin has more pressure than the air you blow, and it lifts the coin up.

1 Hovering ping-pong ball

2

Put some plasticine on one end of a cotton reel, leaving the hole clear. Push four nails into the plasticine. Then put a wide drinking straw (or two narrow ones) into the hole at the other end. Balance the ping-pong ball on the nails and blow up through the straw. The ball hovers just above the reel.

3 How it hovers

STILL AIR

MOVING AIR

When you blow, your breath lifts the ball up and then flows round it. The air stream with the ball inside is held in position by the still air pushing in all round.

Paper trick

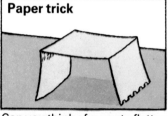

Can you think of a way to flatten this paper using the Bernoulli principle? The answer is on page 61.

How aeroplanes fly

The Bernoulli principle*, which states that moving air has a lower pressure than the air around it, is one of the main reasons why planes can fly. Here is a model wing you can make, to see how the Bernoulli principle works.

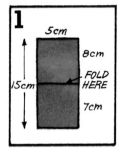

Take a piece of stiff paper 15cm×5cm. Fold the long side 8cm from the end.

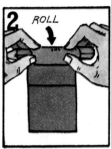

Roll the longer part evenly round a thick pen or pencil to make it bulge.

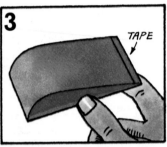

Tape the ends together so the top of the model wing is curved and the bottom is flat as shown. This shape is called an aerofoil.

An aeroplane's wings and tailplane have this special aerofoil shape. Helicopter rotors are shaped like this too.

Testing the model wing

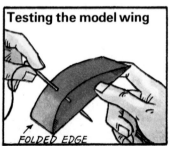

Thread a piece of cotton about 40cm long through the aerofoil, about one third of the way back from the fold.

Hold the cotton tight between both hands and blow straight at the folded edge of the aerofoil. It should move up the cotton.

How an aerofoil works

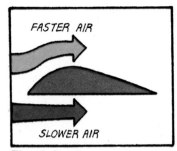

The air flowing over the curved top of the wing travels further and faster than the air below, so it has less pressure.

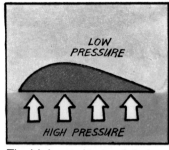

The higher pressure air below pushes the wing up. This is called "lift". It is the main force that keeps a plane in the air.

How a plane takes off

Here are the forces which act on a plane as it takes off.

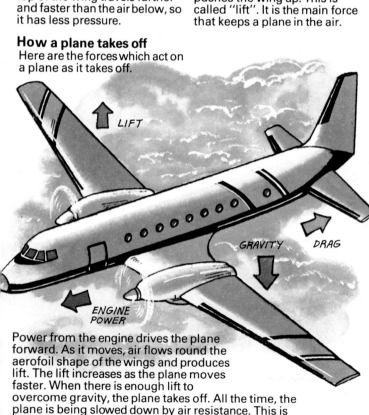

Power from the engine drives the plane forward. As it moves, air flows round the aerofoil shape of the wings and produces lift. The lift increases as the plane moves faster. When there is enough lift to overcome gravity, the plane takes off. All the time, the plane is being slowed down by air resistance. This is called drag and the engine power has to overcome it.

Testing for floaters and sinkers

In this part of the book there are lots of experiments to do to find out how things float. For these you need a large bowl of water – a washing-up bowl or the sink or bath would do – and one or two jam jars.

First try testing things to see whether they float. The list below gives some ideas for things to test, but try anything you can find. Then make a chart of "floaters" and "sinkers".

Ideas for things to test
Ping-pong ball
Marble
Rubber
Empty glass jar with its lid on
Piece of wood
Candle
Plasticine
Nail
Plastic counter
Pumice stone
Coin
Plastic pot (e.g. yogurt pot)
Needle

Something to think about

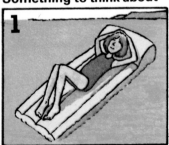

Objects full of air, such as an airbed, or the glass jar with its lid on, are usually good floaters.

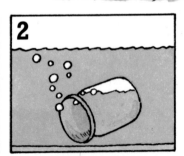

Try taking the lid off the jar and watch it sink as it fills with water. It seems that the air inside was keeping it afloat.

When you have tested everything examine your chart. Do the things which float have anything in common?

A superfloater

See if you can find a polystyrene tray, like those in which meat is sold in supermarkets, and try floating it.

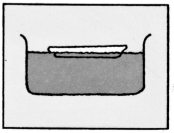

Why do you think it floats so well, hardly sinking into the water at all? It is not just because it is light – a needle is light too, but it sinks.

3

Solid objects though, such as candles and wood, float too. So there must be another reason why things float.

Try loading the tray with coins and watch it float lower and lower in the water. How much load can it carry before sinking?

Making sinkers float

Some materials, such as wood, are natural floaters and some, such as plasticine, are sinkers. It is possible, though, to make sinkers float. You can find out how below.

Find a lump of plasticine about the size of a ping-pong ball and some marbles. Work the plasticine into a hollow bowl-shape, making sure there are no cracks in it.

Now try floating it. If it sinks, try making the sides higher and test it again. Keep adjusting the shape until it floats. Then see how many marbles it can carry.*

Boat designing

Can you redesign the plasticine boat to carry more marbles? Try making the bottom flatter and the sides higher and thinner.

Competition

Give each person an equal amount of plasticine and see whose boat can carry the most marbles.

* *You can find out why the bowl-shape floats over the page.*

Wooden boats and iron boats

BOWL-SHAPED HULL

BRUNEL'S SHIP THE "GREAT EASTERN"

At one time people thought boats could only be made from natural floaters, such as wood. They were amazed when engineers said they could make boats from iron which is a sinker. As with plasticine, iron has to be made into a hollow, bowl-shape in order to make it float.

Iron was better for ship-building than wood because it lasted longer and the ships could be made much bigger. In 1858 an engineer called Brunel built an iron ship 211m long, which at that time was far longer than any other ship in the world.

Candle puzzle

If you float a candle in water like this, how far do you think it can burn down before going out? To find out, cut about 3cm from the top of a candle and push a nail into the bottom. Then try floating it. If it sinks use a lighter nail. If it floats on its side, you need a heavier nail. When it floats upright, light the wick and wait to see what happens. (Answer on page 61.)

WICK MAY TAKE A WHILE TO LIGHT IF IT IS WET

NAIL

How things float

Here is an experiment which shows why a lump of plasticine sinks, but a plasticine bowl-shape floats. To do it, you need to find a large jar with a neck wide enough to fit your hand through.

Put some water in the jar and mark the level with a felt-tip pen. Then drop a lump of plasticine in and mark the level again. You could use a different coloured pen.

The level of the water rises because the ball pushes away, or "displaces" water to make room for itself.

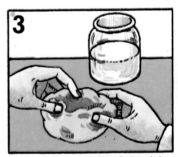

Now make the ball of plasticine into a bowl-shape and float it on the water. Mark the level of the water again.

The level is even higher. This shows that the bowl displaces more water than the ball.

Now put your hand in a plastic bag and dip it in water. You can feel the displaced water pushing against it. A Greek scientist, Archimedes, discovered how this force of water can make things float.

What Archimedes found out

Archimedes lived in Greece over 2,000 years ago. One day he filled his bath too full and when he got in, it overflowed. He did some experiments to find out how much water overflowed and worked out that the amount of water an object displaces is equal to the volume of the object.

Later he worked out that the strength of the force pushing back against an object depends on how much water it displaces.

If an object displaces enough water to make a force strong enough to support its weight, then it floats.

Why the bowl-shape floats

The plasticine bowl and ball weigh the same, but the bowl displaces more water because it is a larger shape. So there is a stronger force pushing against the bowl and this is why it can float.

If you put marbles in the bowl it has to displace more water in order to support the extra weight.

Floating in salty water

Floating is easy in the Dead Sea, which lies between Israel and Jordan. People's bodies hardly sink into the water at all. This is because the water is so salty — seven times saltier than sea water usually is. Below you can find out how to make a special floater which measures how things float in ordinary water and in salty water (often called brine).

Making brine

Pour a jar of warm water (not too hot) into a pan and add salt to it. Stir and keep adding salt until no more will dissolve and it sinks to the bottom.

Leave it for several hours until the liquid is no longer cloudy. If a crust forms, push it to the bottom. Then pour off the clear brine into a labelled jar.

1 Making a special floater

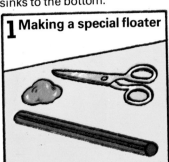

To test the brine, make a special floater from a plastic drinking straw and plasticine.

2

Cut a piece of straw about 6cm long and stick a small lump of plasticine on one end.

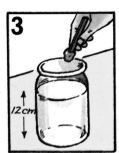

3 Put it in a jar containing at least 12cm of water, to see how it floats.

4 LUMP TOO SMALL

If it topples to one side, make the lump of plasticine bigger. Then test it again.

5 LUMP TOO BIG

If it sinks to the bottom, the lump is too heavy so make it smaller.

6 Adjust it until it floats upright, with part of the straw above the water.

7 Then take it out and dry the straw. Draw a scale on it by laying it alongside a ruler and making marks every 1cm with different coloured pens. Press hard to make clear marks.

Testing water and brine
Now you can use the floater to compare how things float in water and in brine. First see how deep the floater sinks into the water, by noting which mark on the scale the water level comes nearest to. Then see how deep it sinks into the brine. Over the page you can find out why the floater does not sink so far into the brine.

Testing salty water

Things float better in brine than in water, because they do not have to sink so far into it. Here is a test to find out why. You can use the brine left from a previous experiment, or make some as described on page 42. You also need some water, a jam jar, a felt-tip pen and some kitchen scales.

Almost fill the jar with brine and mark the level it comes to. Then put the jar on the kitchen scales and note its weight.

Empty out the brine and fill the jar to the same level with water. Weigh the water. Is it heavier or lighter than the brine?

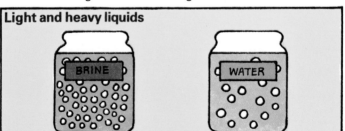

Light and heavy liquids

All substances are made up of particles. In brine the particles are closer together than they are in water, so there are more particles packed into the same space. Therefore if you have the same amount of brine as water, the brine is heavier. It is said to be denser than water.

SPECIAL FLOATER →

The test on the opposite page shows that brine is heavier than water. Because of this, it pushes harder against objects floating in it than water does. So in order to float, things do not have to displace as much brine as they do water. This is why they do not sink so far into brine.

A special floater like the one described on the previous page, which measures how things float in different liquids, is called a hydrometer.

How hydrometers are used

BRINE

WATER

METHYLATED SPIRITS

Scientists use hydrometers to measure how things float in different liquids. This shows them how dense the liquids are. For example, a

hydrometer sinks further in methylated spirits than in water, showing that methylated spirits is less dense than water.

Boatman puzzle

The theory of Archimedes (see page 41) may help you solve this puzzle, or you can try the test below.

A boatman loads his boat with iron bars and rows out into a small pond. Then he dumps the bars overboard. Does the water level in the pond rise, fall, or stay the same?

Test to find the answer

Put some nails in a yogurt pot and float it in a large jar. Mark the water level.

Then tip the nails into the water and refloat the empty pot. What happens to the water level?*

* Answer on page 61.

Loading cargo

Ships which carry cargo have to be carefully designed so that the cargo does not slide about when the ship is in rough water. To see what could happen to a ship with "shifting" cargo, try making a paper boat as shown below, then float it and load it with marbles.

Can you think of a way to stop the marbles rolling to one end? The section below about tankers may give you an idea.

How to make a paper boat

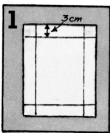

1 On a piece of paper, draw lines like this 3cm in from the edges. Fold along the lines.

3cm

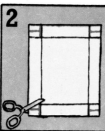

2 Make two cuts at each corner along the lines shown here in red, to make tabs.

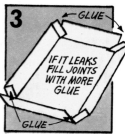

3 Bend the sides up and stick the tabs to the ends with waterproof glue.

GLUE

IF IT LEAKS FILL JOINTS WITH MORE GLUE

GLUE

Tankers

Tankers are specially designed with very large holds for carrying oil and other chemicals.

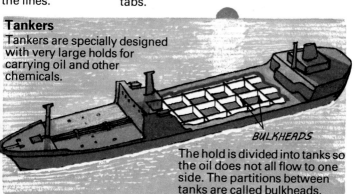

BULKHEADS

The hold is divided into tanks so the oil does not all flow to one side. The partitions between tanks are called bulkheads.

Egg trick

If you put an egg in water, it sinks to the bottom. Can you work out how to make it float half-way up a jar, like the one shown here?

You can find out how to do it below. Then you could try the trick on your friends, to see if they can work it out.

Make some brine, as on page 42, by stirring salt into warm water. Leave it to settle for several hours, then pour off the clear brine.

Half fill a wide-necked jar, or glass jug, with brine and put a fresh egg into it. It should float, even if you push it under.

POUR WATER AGAINST SIDE OF JAR

Tilt the jar and *very gently* pour water into it until it is full. Now the egg should be floating half-way up the jar.

How it works

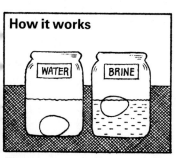

The egg floats in brine but not in water because brine is denser than water and can support the egg's weight.

Water, as it is less dense, also floats on brine. So in fact, both the egg and the water are floating on the brine.

Test to prove it

Colour some water with a few drops of ink. Then gently pour it on to some brine in a jar, by tilting the jar as you did before. Take care not to pour too hard, or the brine and water will mix.

Did you know?

A ship floats at different levels depending on the weight of its cargo and the kind of water it is sailing through. It floats lower in fresh river water than in salty sea water, and also in warm water which is less dense than cold.

Every ship has a special mark on the side, to show how deeply the fully-loaded ship should float in different kinds of water.

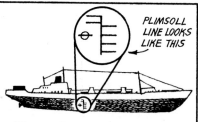

PLIMSOLL LINE LOOKS LIKE THIS

The mark is called the Plimsoll Line, after Samuel Plimsoll. He introduced it in 1885, to protect sailors from shipowners who loaded so much cargo on to their ships that they were likely to sink.

Special floaters

If you drop a needle in water, it sinks. It is so small it cannot push away enough water to support its weight. It is possible, though, to make a needle float right on top of the surface of the water. Can you work out how?

How to do it

Put some water into a clean bowl or jar. Make sure the needle is dry, then rest it across a fork. Lower the needle gently on to the water and pull the fork out carefully.

How it works

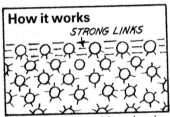

STRONG LINKS

Water, like everything else, is made up of tiny particles, called molecules. The molecules at the surface are more strongly linked than those below and act like a kind of skin. This is called surface tension.

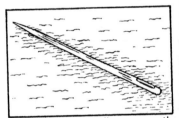

If you put the needle very gently on to the water, it rests on top of the surface. You can probably see that the surface is dented where the needle is lying.

Walking on water

Have you ever seen an insect skating across the surface of a pond? Like the needle, it is supported by the surface tension of the water. You may see round hollows where the insect's feet press down the surface of the water.

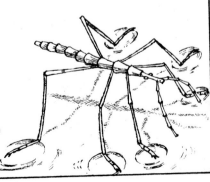

A speedboat to make

To make this simple boat which speeds across the surface of the water, you need some thin card and washing-up liquid.

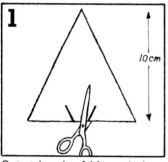

1 10cm

Cut a triangle of thin card, about 10cm long, and make two small cuts in the base as shown.

2 FLAP

Bend up the flap between the cuts and then float the boat in some clean, shallow water.

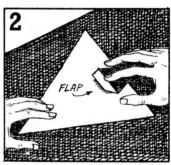

3 TOUCH HERE

Put a drop of washing-up liquid on your finger and touch the water in the gap at the back of the boat with it. The boat should shoot forward.

How it works

Washing-up liquid stops the molecules at the surface clinging together and so decreases the surface tension of the water.

The boat is resting on the surface of the water and the drop of washing-up liquid at the back decreases the tension there. The boat is pulled forward by the stronger tension at the front. To do it again you need fresh water and a new boat.

Pen-top diver

Here is how to make a pen-top dive like a submarine to the bottom of a bottle and come back up again. You need a plastic pen-top, some metal paper-clips, a candle and a plastic bottle with a screw-cap.

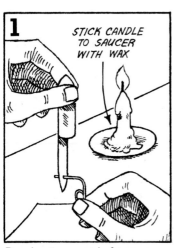

1 STICK CANDLE TO SAUCER WITH WAX

Bend out one end of a paper-clip and heat it in a candle flame. Then use the hot wire to melt a hole in the pen-top as shown here.

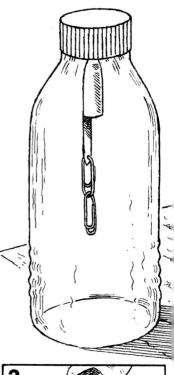

2 PUT CANDLE OUT →

Put the candle out. Then push a new paper-clip through the hole in the pen-top and hook another clip to it, to make a chain.

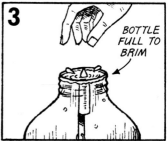

3 BOTTLE FULL TO BRIM

Fill the bottle with water and drop the pen-top in. It should float with the tip just showing. If it sinks use a smaller paper-clip.

How it works

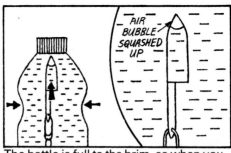

When you put the diver in water, an air bubble is trapped inside it.

The bottle is full to the brim, so when you squeeze it, the water has nowhere to go. It pushes further into the diver and squashes the air bubble into a smaller space.

4

Now screw the cap on tightly and squeeze the bottle. The "diver" should go right down to the bottom of the bottle and come back up when you stop squeezing.

If it does not work, you may need to add another paper-clip to the pen-top so it does not float so well. Make sure, too, that the bottle is full to the brim.

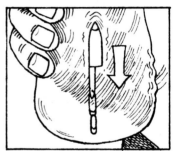

Now there is more water in the diver so it is heavier. This makes it too heavy to float, so it sinks to the bottom of the bottle.

When you relax the pressure, the air bubble expands and pushes the extra water out of the diver, so it is lighter and comes up again.

53

How a submarine works

A submarine can dive under water and come up to the surface again by altering its weight. To do this it has big tanks called ballast tanks, which can be filled and emptied. You can find out how they work below.

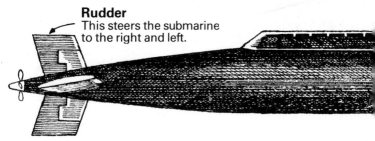

Rudder
This steers the submarine to the right and left.

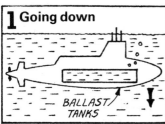

1 Going down

BALLAST TANKS

The ballast tanks are filled with water through flood holes in the bottom of the tanks and the air is forced out. This makes the submarine heavier, so it sinks.

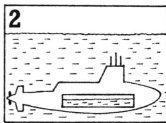

2

To stop the submarine sinking, air is pumped back into the tanks to push out some of the water and make the submarine lighter.

3

TRIM TANKS

As the submarine uses up fuel and other supplies, it becomes lighter. To make up for this it has another set of tanks, called trim tanks, which are filled with water to replace the weight lost.

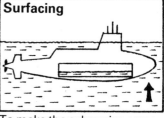

Surfacing

To make the submarine come up again, more air is pumped into the ballast tanks and most of the water is pushed out. This makes the submarine light enough to float, so it rises.

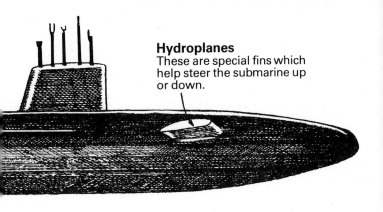

Hydroplanes
These are special fins which help steer the submarine up or down.

How hydroplanes work

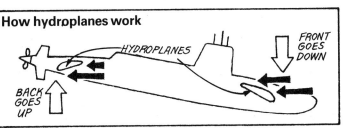

HYDROPLANES

FRONT GOES DOWN

BACK GOES UP

To dive, the rear hydroplanes are raised, so water pressing underneath them forces the back of the submarine up. The front hydroplanes are dipped, so water pressing on top of them forces the front down.

Why a hot air balloon is like a submarine

A hot air balloon is like a submarine floating in an ocean of air.

The balloon is filled with hot air, which is less dense and so lighter than the cooler air around it. This makes the balloon rise. When the air in the balloon cools, it gets heavier and sinks, just like a submarine with its ballast tanks full of water.

Emergency floaters

Knowing the best way to float could help you in an emergency. For instance, a person afraid of drowning usually panics and waves his arms about. This only makes it more difficult to float, though. To find out why, try making a dummy body as shown below and testing it with its arms in different positions. You will need a metal tube with a cap, such as a cigar tube, a clothes peg, plasticine and a rubber band.

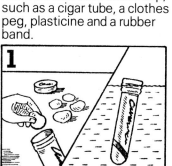

1 Put some plasticine in the tube, screw the cap on and try floating it. Add or take out plasticine until it floats with the top just level with the water.

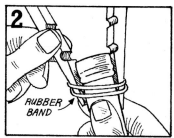

2 To make "arms", wind a rubber band round the top of the tube, then pull a peg apart and push the bits of peg under the band, so they stick upwards.

RUBBER BAND

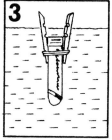

3 Float the dummy with its arms in this position. Its top goes underwater.

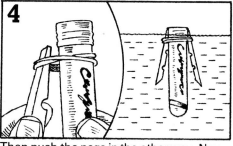

4 Then push the pegs in the other way. Now the arms are under the water and the dummy displaces more water, so it floats a little better. This also happens with a real body.

Life-saver puzzle

Here is a puzzle to see how many life-savers you can spot.

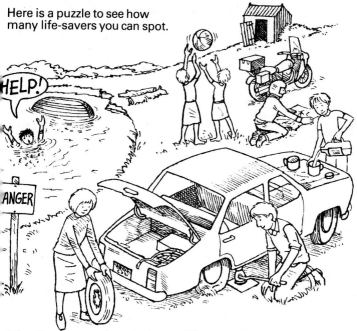

A family, out on a day-trip, has stopped by a lake to change a punctured wheel on the car. One of the children takes a boat out on to the lake, then leans over too far and topples in.

The water is deep and the boy is in danger of drowning, but nobody can swim. Look in the picture to see how many things there are which could be used to save him. (Answer on page 61.)

Breathing and floating

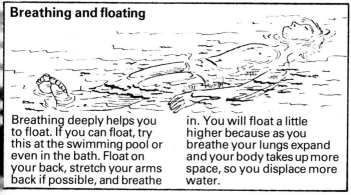

Breathing deeply helps you to float. If you can float, try this at the swimming pool or even in the bath. Float on your back, stretch your arms back if possible, and breathe in. You will float a little higher because as you breathe your lungs expand and your body takes up more space, so you displace more water.

Weight and weightlessness

Below there is an experiment you can do to show that falling things are weightless.

When you pick up a bag of potatoes, what you feel as weight is the force you are using to resist the pull of gravity on the bag. If you let the bag fall, it is no longer resisting the pull of gravity so it becomes weightless. In the same way, a parachutist who jumps from a plane and starts falling is weightless.

The parachutist is weightless until his parachute opens and resists the pull of gravity on him.

1 Experiment

Put a brick, or a heavy book, on a pair of bathroom scales and note the weight. Then hold them over a soft bed.

2

Watching the weight-reading all the time, drop the scales with the book on top, on to the bed. What happens to the weight?

Explanation

As the scales fall towards the bed, the reading swings right back below zero. The book has become weightless because it is falling and no longer resisting gravity.

As soon as everything hits the bed, gravity is being resisted again and the book weighs the same as before.

How astronauts lose weight

Below you can find out why astronauts in a satellite float weightless in their cabin.

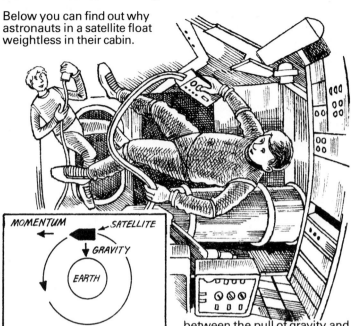

A satellite moves at a constant speed because there is no air to slow it down. This movement is called momentum. Momentum drives the satellite forward but gravity constantly pulls it towards the earth. The balance between the pull of gravity and the drive of momentum keeps the satellite in orbit round the earth. The satellite and the astronauts are not resisting the pull of gravity. They are falling freely like the parachutist, so they are weightless.

Lift puzzle

Imagine you are standing on some scales in a lift. What happens to the weight-reading as the lift goes down? The experiment on the opposite page may help you solve this puzzle.
The answer is on page 61.

Ice-cube puzzle

This ice-cube is floating in a glass full of water. What do you think will happen when the ice-cube melts? Will the glass overflow?

Before you look at the answer on the opposite page, try the experiment below – it may give you a clue.

1 Experiment

Put some water in a paper or plastic cup and mark the level with a felt-tip pen. Then put it in the freezer and leave it for several hours.

2

When it is frozen, check the level. It should be higher now, because water expands when it freezes. What happens to the level when the ice melts again?

Icebergs

Only about one tenth of an iceberg shows above the sea. This is because when water freezes and changes to ice, it takes up about one tenth more space than it did as water.

The hidden part of icebergs can be very dangerous to ships, as they can be torn open by the jagged, underwater ice peaks.

Puzzle answers

Paper helicopter
(Page 10)

The helicopter needs shorter rotors to trap less air.

Paper trick
(Page 33)
Blow through the paper arch so the higher pressure above it pushes it down.

Boatman puzzle
(Page 46)
With the iron bars in, the boat pushes away a lot of water. The bars by themselves only push away a little water. So when they are dumped in the pond the level goes down. Is this what your test showed?

Candle puzzle
(Page 39)
The candle can burn right down because it gets lighter. This makes it float higher in the water so the flame does not get wet.

Aerobatic puzzles (Page 23)

◀ To loop the loop, bend both elevons up slightly and launch steeply up.

To dive and turn ▶ upside-down, bend both elevons right down and launch steeply down.

◀ To turn sharply, bend one elevon half up and the other a quarter up. Launch slightly down.

Life-saver puzzle
(Page 57)
The logs of wood, large, empty squash bottle with its cap on, spare wheel, loose shed door, beach ball or empty plastic luggage box from the motorbike could be thrown in to help the boy float. Or he could cling to the upturned boat (which floats because it traps air). Then the rope or danger sign could be used to pull him out.

Lift puzzle
(Page 59)
As the lift goes down, the weight-reading swings back towards zero. The faster the lift goes down, the less it is resisting gravity and the more the reading swings back.

Ice-cube puzzle
(page 60)
When the ice-cube melts, the water level in the glass stays about the same. This is because the water from the ice takes up less space than the ice itself.

Pattern for Mark 2 glider

Here is the pattern for the glider on page 24. Fold the paper you are using to make the glider as shown on page 24. Then trace all the lines of this pattern on to the paper, making sure that the bottom line is along the fold, as shown.

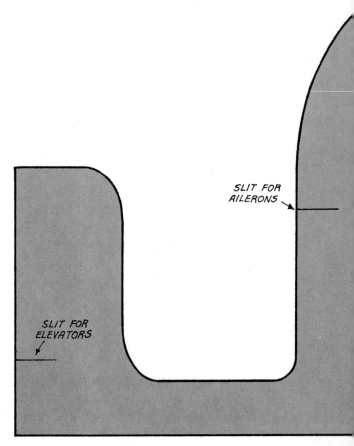

SLIT FOR AILERONS

SLIT FOR ELEVATORS

PLACE THIS LINE ALONG
FOLD IN PAPER

Index